First published in Great Britain in 2012 by Boxer Books Limited.

www.boxerbooks.com

Based on an original idea by Sam Williams.

Monstrous Stories™ concept, names, stories, designs and logos
© Boxer Books Limited

Written by Paul Harrison
Paul Harrison asserts his moral right to be identified
as the author of this work.
Text copyright © 2012 Boxer Books Limited

Illustrated by Tom Knight
Tom Knight asserts his moral right to be identified
as the illustrator of this work.
Illustrations copyright © 2012 Tom Knight

The illustrations were prepared using brush, ink and digital.
The text is set in Blackmoor Plain and Adobe Caslon.

ISBN 978-1-907967-34-4
1 3 5 7 9 10 8 6 4 2

Printed and bound by CPI Group (UK) Ltd, Croydon, CR0 4YY

All of our papers are sourced from
managed forests and renewable resources.

Dr Roach's Monstrous STORIES

Dr Roach presents

ATTACK OF THE GIANT HAMSTER

a Boxer Books production

Contents

Dr Roach welcomes YOU!

Have you seen those ads that say they will make you beautiful, slim, give you big muscles and even more hair? Pish-posh, I say – it's all make-believe. Or is it?

Our story is about Hercules. No, not the mighty Greek God – but a pet hamster called Hercules. He isn't strong. He is a small, fluffy, lazy little hamstery slob.

How amazing, then, that Hercules is able to scare the townsfolk, crush cars and trample the farmers' market in search of some delicious food.

How, you ask? Come closer, my friend, and I'll tell you all about it.

Welcome to Dr Roach's Monstrous Stories. Enjoy!

Chapter 1
Hairy, Fat and Useless!

Hercules the hamster was quite possibly the world's laziest pet.

Billy Philips sat in the living room, watching his hamster do what it did best – nothing. Billy had pestered his parents for ages for a hamster. Now that he had one, it was a massive disappointment. Hercules would sleep for most of the day and then occasionally wake up and waddle over to his food bowl. And that was as exciting as it got.

Billy reached into the cage and lowered Hercules onto his exercise wheel. Hercules sat there with a piece of lettuce sticking out of his mouth.

"Come on then," said Billy, "move."

Hercules stared at Billy and slowly started chewing.

"You are a hairy, fat, useless slob," said Billy in disgust.

Hercules seemed to smile. Billy
sighed and switched on the TV.

"Has your get-up-and-go got up
and left?" said a voice on the TV.
There was an image of an old lady
snoozing in a chair. "Has all your
vim vamoosed?" continued the voice-
over man. "Then you need Booster
Bites – the power snack that puts the
power back!"

Now the old lady was bouncing across the screen.

"That's what you need, Hercules," muttered Billy.

"Try Booster Bites today, and if you're not happy, we'll refund your money," the advert promised.

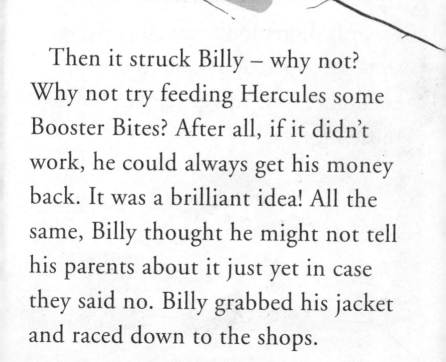

Then it struck Billy – why not?
Why not try feeding Hercules some
Booster Bites? After all, if it didn't
work, he could always get his money
back. It was a brilliant idea! All the
same, Billy thought he might not tell
his parents about it just yet in case
they said no. Billy grabbed his jacket
and raced down to the shops.

Chapter 2
Booster Bites

When Billy got home, he crushed a couple of Booster Bites into some of Hercules' dry food. It didn't look very appetising, so he chopped a bit of lettuce and cucumber into tiny pieces and mixed those in, too.

"Perfect," said Billy.

He put it down next to Hercules.

"Lunchtime, Hercules!"

Hercules sniffed the bowl lazily.

Then, to Billy's joy, he tucked right in.

"This is good. This is very good,"
thought Billy.

Billy sat and watched Hercules

to see if anything would happen.
Hercules just sat in a little, fat, furry
heap and stared right back.

Billy stared at Hercules.

Hercules stared at Billy.

Then Hercules fell asleep.

"Typical!" huffed Billy. He stomped
off to the kitchen to fix himself
some lunch.

Billy wandered back into the room with a sandwich and a drink. He glanced over at Hercules – and stopped in his tracks! Was it his imagination or was Hercules bigger than before? Yes, yes, Hercules was definitely bigger and awake.

Billy did a little jig of delight, but stopped very quickly. Hercules had grown again. The hamster was now three times its normal size.

A terrible thought struck Billy: how would he explain this to his parents? He began to panic.

He looked at Hercules again – he
was still growing. There was no other
choice – Billy had to hide him. Billy
scooped up the cage and charged
upstairs. Then he wondered what to
do next.

Chapter 3
Panic!

In a panic, Billy dashed back to the kitchen and grabbed the box of Booster Bites. Frantically, he read the back, looking for something that might explain what was happening to Hercules. Nothing – but there was a telephone number for customer services.

Billy dialled the number.

"Hello, Booster Bites customer services, how can I help you?" said a woman's voice.

"Hi," Billy replied, "I think your Booster Bites are making my hamster grow."

"You fed them to your hamster?" the women said.

"Ermmm, yes …"

"And they're making it grow?"

"Yes," Billy replied.

"Well, Booster Bites are a nutritious snack …"

"My hamster is three times his size! And he's still growing!"

"Oh. Well, we don't recommend that Booster Bites are fed to animals," said the voice.

"It doesn't say that on the packet!" said Billy, panicking.

"Really? Are you sure your hamster is actually growing? It's not just fluffed itself up a bit?" said the woman.

"Fluffed up? He looks like a hairy balloon!" said Billy.

"Is this some kind of joke?"

"No, no, no; there's something wrong with my hamster," said Billy.

"Hmm. Well, I suppose we could send a scientist down to have a look tomorrow ..." The woman sounded doubtful.

"Great, thank you, thank you,

thank you!"

Before the woman could change her mind, Billy gave her his address and put the phone down.

Chapter 4
Hamster Dung

Knowing help was on the way made Billy feel better. He dashed back upstairs to check on Hercules. That made him feel worse. Hercules had gotten so big he burst out of his cage. Where could Billy hide him now? Billy raised his eyes upwards, searching for inspiration. And there it was, right above him – the loft!

 The only way
Billy could get
him up the ladder
was by putting
Hercules over
his shoulder, like
a really heavy
beanbag.

Billy just got the loft door closed
when his parents arrived home. "Hi
Billy, we're back. Everything okay,
sweetie?" called his mother.

"Sure … fine, Mum," Billy replied,
casting a nervous glance upwards.

The rest of the day was difficult.
Hercules continued to grow. By
the afternoon he was the size of a
cow. The bigger Hercules got, the

hungrier he seemed to be. Billy had to smuggle more and more food up to the loft.

However, there was a bigger and smellier problem. A huge Hercules did massive poos.

"And I thought cleaning your cage out was bad," grumbled Billy as he shovelled great lumps of hamster dung into rubbish bags.

Hercules just looked at Billy and chomped down another lettuce.

The poo couldn't stay in the loft. Billy had to carry it downstairs and flush it down the toilet. All these trips to the bathroom were not going unnoticed.

"You feeling okay, sweetie?" his mum asked.

"I'm fine, Mum," Billy fibbed.

By bedtime, the toilet was blocked. As Billy's dad, Herman, struggled to unblock the toilet, grumbling about how much a plumber would cost, Billy counted down the hours until tomorrow.

Chapter 5
Prof. Heinzwinkel

The new day brought more bad
news. The ceiling above Billy's
bedroom was bulging downwards.
How long would it be before his
parents noticed, Billy wondered. But
luckily they were too busy wondering
why the refrigerator was empty.

"What have you done with all the carrots, Herman?" asked Billy's mum.

"Carrots? What carrots?" replied Billy's dad.

"The lettuce is gone, too," yelled Billy's mum. "Any ideas, Billy?"

"Erm ..." Billy tried to think of something to say.

Ding dong! There was someone at the door.

He was saved by the bell.

"Ah, that must be the plumber," said Billy's dad, going for the door.

"Good morning, my name is Professor Eric von Heinzwinkel," said the visitor.

"Professor? That's highly qualified for a plumber," said Billy's dad.

"Plumber? I'm here about the hamster," replied the professor.

"Hamster?" said Billy's dad.

"He's come to see Hercules," said Billy, taking the professor by the arm and dragging him upstairs.

"Am I glad to see you," said Billy.

He opened the loft door, but they couldn't get in as Hercules was filling the entire space.

"Billy! What's going on up there?" his dad called.

Ding dong!

Once again the doorbell came to the rescue.

"Are you another professor?" asked Billy's dad.

"No, I'm a plumber. But I reckon you need someone to fix your roof."

"What's wrong with the roof?" said Billy's dad.

Just then a roof tile smashed to the ground.

Billy's mum and dad raced outside. Tiles were falling off the roof and gingery fur was poking out.

"BILLY!" shouted his dad.

Chapter 6
Falling Down

CREAAAAKKKKKK!
GRRRROOOAAAAANNNNN!

Billy and the professor charged out
of the house – straight into Billy's
parents and the plumber.

"Billy Philips, I demand to know
what is going on – right now!"
shouted his dad.

"I ... well ... it's difficult to explain ..." stammered Billy.

"Try me," his dad replied.

Just then a massive crash came from the house.

"What on earth was that?" said Billy's mum.

"I'll pay for any damage!" cried Billy.

The house began to shudder.

Billy, his parents, the plumber and the professor moved further away from the house. Hercules had just crashed through the ceiling and was growing at an enormous rate. With a terrible crunching sound, the walls of the house were pushed out and came crashing to the ground in a massive cloud of dust.

"Billy," said his dad, "on your pocket money you'll be paying for this damage until the year 3000."

The dust slowly cleared, revealing a giant-sized Hercules sitting where the house used to be.

The roof sat on Hercules' head at a jaunty angle like a hat. The hamster blinked a couple of times, as if it had just woken up, and yawned. It shook itself free of the debris and started munching on the plants in the Philips' garden.

"That … that …" Billy's mum struggled to find the right words.

"… is Hercules," said Billy.

"Do I take it you don't need me anymore?" said the plumber – and without waiting for an answer ran for his van.

"I'd better be off too," said Professor Heinzwinkel. "I need to get some stuff from my lab. I'll be back as soon as I can. Don't let him out of your sight."

"Well, that's hardly likely," said Billy's dad. "Look at the size of him!"

Just then, Hercules sniffed the air – something had got his attention. Abruptly, he got up and waddled down the street, squashing cars and knocking over street lamps as he went.

"Where's Hercules going?" shouted Billy's dad.

"He's heading for town," cried Billy.

"Of course! THE FRUIT AND VEG MARKET!" wailed his mum.

For a moment, the Philipses stopped and thought about what would happen when a huge, hungry hamster came face to face with a market stuffed with its favourite food. It was not a pleasant thought – unless of course you were a hamster. Then it was the stuff of dreams …

Chapter 7
Call the Army

Hercules could hardly believe his podgy cheeks when he saw all the vegetables. The people in the market couldn't believe their eyes when they saw a twenty metre high hamster descending on them.

"ARGGGHGHHH!" they cried and scattered in all directions. Hercules ignored them and filled his face with food.

By the time the Philips family arrived, Hercules had eaten everything in sight and was settling down for a lengthy snooze.

"What now?" asked Billy's dad.

"We wait for the professor," said Billy.

"Excuse me – is that your hamster?"

Billy turned around. There was a
police officer standing there.

"Yes, that's my pet, Hercules," Billy
replied.

"You've got some explaining to do,
son."

While Billy tried to explain the
unexplainable, a lot was going on.

First, the police roped off the area
to keep people away. Then, as night
fell, helicopters whirred overhead
and there was a rumble of trucks and
tanks as the army circled the area.

"What's going on?" Billy asked,
turning to his dad.

"It's Hercules, son," his dad replied. "The army are going to deal with him in the morning."

"No one's shooting my pet!" shouted Billy. He ducked under the police rope and went straight to the general leading the army.

"You can't do this," said Billy.

"Oh, yes we can, sonny," the general replied.

"But the professor is coming with a cure!" Billy pleaded.

The general looked at his watch.

"How long will your hamster sleep for?" asked the general.

"Normally until breakfast time," Billy replied.

"Well then," the general said. "Your professor has got until 7.30am to get here. If he's not, then we go in."

Chapter 8
Hold your Nose!

It was a warm night, so Billy, his mum and dad all spent the night nearby in a police tent with police sleeping bags. But Billy didn't sleep a wink. Partly that was from worry, but mainly because Hercules had been snoring. Billy wasn't the only one kept awake. The general was pacing up and down by the rope in a foul temper.

"Right, we can't risk the hamster waking up – I'm sending in the troops now."

"But it's only 7 o'clock!" shouted Billy.

"Hello, hello, good morning!" said a new voice.

"Who on earth …?" said the general.

"I am Professor Heinzwinkel. Hello Billy – glad to see you kept an eye on Hercules for me. Now, not a moment to spare – pop this into Hercules' mouth."

The professor gave Billy a large
tablet. Billy put a large lettuce round
it, raced straight over to Hercules
and slipped it into the hamster's
mouth.

"What happens now?" asked Billy.

"I'm not entirely sure ..." the
professor admitted.

For a moment, nothing happened. Then Hercules opened his eyes wide, looking alarmed. Then he began to get bigger and rounder by the second.

"He's growing again," cried the general. "I'm sending in the tanks!"

"No, wait!" said the professor. "It's the tablet working. It's turning all the growth into gas."

Hercules now looked like a giant, furry football.

"But how will the gas get out?" asked Billy.

"One of two ways ..." the professor began.

Hercules' body tensed up and his eyes went crossed. Then, with an almighty trump, he shot into the air like a rocket.

Hercules sped this way and that through the sky like a balloon that had been let go.

He crashed into a mobile phone tower and bounced off buildings, all the while getting smaller and smaller.

After a minute or so he was back
to normal size and fell gently down
towards the ground, where he was
caught by a grateful Billy.

"Good, good," said Professor
Heinzwinkel. "Everything is back to
normal."

"Thanks, professor!" said Billy.
"From now on, I don't care how lazy
Hercules is!"

"Yes, just keep him off the Booster Bites and all will be good."

And everything did feel good. Apart from the damaged buildings, and the flattened street lamps, and the crushed cars, of course.

Oh yes, and the terrible smell of hamster gas.

Do you have goldfish? Such ordinary little creatures - and quite boring really. Imagine how much more exciting they would be if they were huge and had legs. Now that would make them more interesting pets, don't you think?

Let's meet Judd Crank and his friend Zak. Two ordinary boys, in an ordinary town, with some very ordinary goldfish.

Who would have thought that those little goldfish would become great monsters and step right out of their tank and into town - looking for trouble?

How, you ask? Get a copy today and I'll tell you everything!

Catch you later!

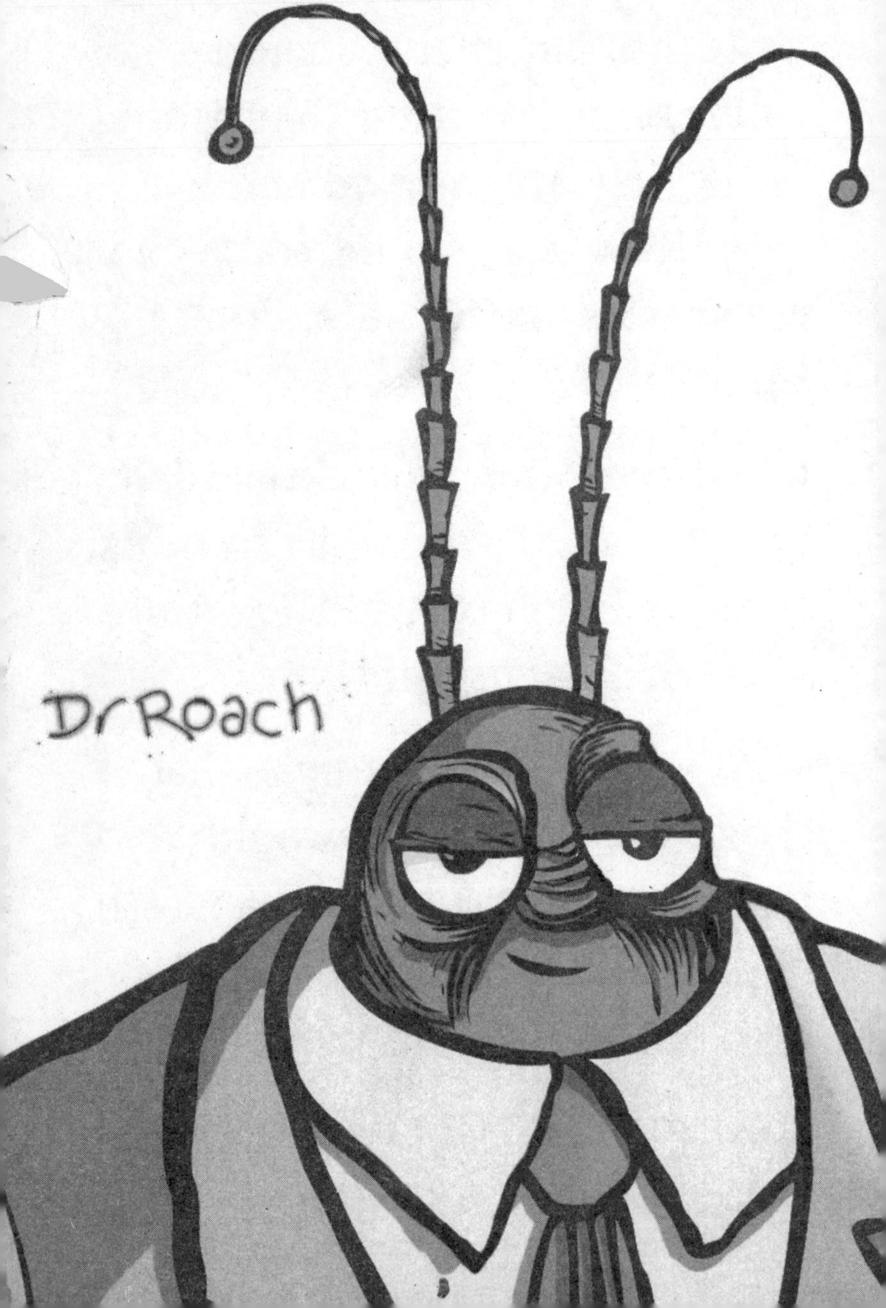